D0531896

179183

Drive to the HOOP

BY JAKE MADDOX

text by Val Priebe

illustrated by Pulsar Studio
(Beehive)

STONE ARCH BOOKS
a capstone imprint

Jake Maddox books are published by Stone Arch Books
A Capstone Imprint
1710 Roe Crest Drive
North Mankato, Minnesota 56003
www.capstonepub.com

*Library of Congress Cataloging-in-Publication Data is available on
the Library of Congress website.*

ISBN: 978-1-4342-2500-9 (library binding)

Summary: Not everyone is happy when Mel moves up to the JV
basketball team, especially her old teammates.

Art Director/Graphic Designer: Kay Fraser
Image Manipulation: Sean Tiffany
Production Specialist: Michelle Biedscheid

Printed in the United States of America in Stevens Point, Wisconsin.
092011
006391R

Table of CONTENTS

CHAPTER 1
Bad News. 5

CHAPTER 2
Good News and Bad News 10

CHAPTER 3
Visiting 17

CHAPTER 4
The Worst Practice Ever. 23

CHAPTER 5
"Everybody Hates Me!". 31

CHAPTER 6
A New Friend. 35

CHAPTER 7
Try, Try Again. 40

CHAPTER 8
New Girl. 47

CHAPTER 9
Setting Goals 53

CHAPTER 10
A Team. 59

· CHAPTER 1 ·
Bad News

Mel was sick of warming up alone at basketball practice. Sometimes she warmed up with Leslie, the point guard on the junior varsity team. But today, Leslie was gone. That meant Mel would be warming up all by herself.

Mel, her mom, and her older sister, Emily, had moved to Springfield right before the school year started. Four months later, Mel still didn't have many friends.

Emily had joined the cheerleading squad and made friends right away. But Mel barely knew anyone. Being on the Springfield Bears basketball team was the only thing stopping her from running back to Green Prairie and her old friends.

As soon as the team had finished warming up and stretching, Coach Arnold, the junior-varsity coach, had everyone sit down together at half court.

"Girls, I have to tell you some bad news," the coach said. "Leslie was in a car accident last night."

All of the players got quiet. Coach Arnold went on, "She's going to be okay, but she won't be able to play basketball for the rest of the season. Today, I will be having a tryout with the freshman players to fill Leslie's JV spot."

Mel felt like she had been punched in the stomach. She looked around the gym. A lot of her teammates had tears streaming down their faces. Everyone was friends with Leslie. She was one of the nicest girls on the JV team. And she was one of the few people who was really friendly to Mel.

Coach Arnold interrupted the silence in the gym. "Girls, I know this is bad news," she said. "But Leslie's going to be okay. So let's practice hard today. After we're done, I'll give the hospital information to anyone who wants to go visit Leslie." A few people nodded.

Mel's stomach did flips. Today wasn't a regular practice. It was a tryout, to play on the JV team for the rest of the season. And since Leslie and Mel were both point guards, Mel actually had a shot.

But Mel knew Leslie was really good. The JV team was really going to miss her. Mel made up her mind. She'd try as hard as she could during the tryout.

Maybe Coach Arnold will even pick me! she thought.

Mel felt a little guilty about being excited about the chance to play on the JV team. After all, Leslie was hurt, and she was in the hospital. But she was going to be okay. Mel knew she might never get a chance like this again.

The first drill of the tryout was called Zig Zag. Mel was paired up with Felicia. The other girl was supposed to play defense and try to steal the ball from Mel while she dribbled up the court. At half court, Mel was supposed to try to dribble in and make a lay-up.

Mel knew that she was a little faster than Felicia, so at half court, she put on a burst of speed and drove to the basket. *Swish!*

Then it was Mel's turn to play defense. Felicia was pretty good at dribbling, but Mel managed to poke the ball away and stop her from making her lay-up.

"Good job," Mel said as both girls jogged to the end of the line. Felicia glared at her.

"What did I do?" Mel murmured. "I'm just trying my best."

CHAPTER 2

Good News and Bad News

After practice, Coach Arnold and Coach Gregg, the freshman coach, huddled together. Mel knew they were talking about the tryout.

Finally, Coach Arnold blew her whistle. "Okay, girls!" she called. "We have made our decision."

Everyone gathered around the coaches. Mel could feel her heart pounding. *I hope I made it,* she thought.

Coach Arnold said, "Based on today's tryout and all of her hard work this season, Mel Hones will be moved up to junior varsity for the rest of this season."

A few girls clapped. Felicia shot Mel a dirty look. But no one else seemed to notice.

"Good job, Mel," said Coach Arnold. "Everyone was great today. It was a tough decision to make. See you all tomorrow!"

No one talked to Mel in the locker room that day. She missed her old school. There, if she'd gotten to play on the JV team, all of her friends would have celebrated with her.

* * *

When she got home from practice, Mel headed to her sister's room.

"What's up?" Emily asked, looking up from her math textbook.

Mel took a deep breath. "I have good news and bad news," she said. "Leslie got into a car accident. She's in the hospital." She added, "That's the bad news."

Emily gave her a sad smile and nodded. "I heard about it," Emily said. "Her sister is really upset, but she said Leslie's going to be fine. We can go to the hospital and see her if you want to."

"Um, yeah, maybe," Mel said.

"What's the good news?" Emily asked.

"We had tryouts at practice today to fill Leslie's spot on junior varsity," Mel answered. "The coaches picked me!"

"That's great!" Emily said, smiling. "Have you told Mom yet?"

Mel shook her head.

"Well, what are you waiting for?" her sister asked. "Come on!"

Emily and Mel raced up to their mom's home office and burst through the door.

"What's going on?" Mom asked, frowning. "Is everything okay? You guys scared me."

Mel explained what had happened to Leslie. "Leslie's going to be okay," she finished. "But she can't play for the rest of the year. So after Coach Arnold told us about Leslie's accident, she announced that all the freshmen were going to try out for Leslie's spot on the JV team."

"A surprise tryout, huh?" Mom said. "How did it go?"

"I'm the new JV point guard!" Mel said happily.

Mom hugged Mel. "I know moving to a new town and starting a new school hasn't been easy on you," Mom said. "But you're doing so great! I'm very proud of you!"

"Thanks, Mom," said Mel.

"Let's celebrate," Emily said. "Pizza Palace!"

"Great idea. Mel gets to pick the toppings," Mom said. "I'll get my coat. Meet you in the car."

"We should go see Leslie after school tomorrow," Emily said as she and Mel put on their coats. "We can go before basketball practice."

Mel swallowed nervously. She was a little scared to see Leslie. How would Leslie feel about being replaced on the team? What if she was mad at Mel for taking her spot?

But on the other hand, Leslie was one of the few girls who had been friendly to Mel. And Mel knew that if she was in the hospital, Leslie would have come to see her.

"Okay," Mel said slowly. "It'll be good for her to have visitors."

· CHAPTER 3 ·
Visiting

The next day before basketball practice, Emily and Mel headed to the hospital. They stopped at a florist on the way and picked up some pretty flowers and a "Get Well Soon" card.

When they got to Leslie's room, Mel saw that there were a lot of tubes and wires everywhere and a computer monitor in the corner of the room. Leslie's right leg was in a cast all the way up to her hip.

Leslie was in bed. Her face broke into a big smile when she saw the two sisters standing in the doorway.

Mel followed Emily into the room. She felt guilty about walking around, playing basketball, and going to school when Leslie was stuck in a giant cast in a hospital bed.

"It's so nice to see you guys," Leslie said. "Thank you so much for coming!"

Emily gave her a hug. "I'm glad you're okay," she said. "We wanted to come and see how you were."

Mel nodded. "It's good to see you," she said quietly. "How are you feeling?"

Before Leslie could answer, Emily headed for the door. "I think I'm going to grab a cup of coffee," she said. "I'll be back in a minute."

After Emily left, Leslie raised an eyebrow and looked at Mel.

"I'm not contagious, you know," Leslie said with a half-smile.

"Uh, I know," Mel said. She inched closer to the bed.

"I heard you're taking my spot on the JV team," Leslie said. "Coach Arnold came by last night."

"I bet you've had a lot of visitors, huh?" Mel said.

Leslie shrugged. "Actually, no," she said. She smiled. "I think a lot of people are scared of hospitals. It was really nice of you to come."

Mel was silent for a moment. "Are you mad at me for taking your spot?" she asked quietly.

Leslie laughed. "No way!" she said. She pointed at her cast. "It's not like I can play with this thing on," she said. "And anyway, I heard you were great at the tryout. Someone has to take my spot, so I'm glad it's you."

The block of ice that had been forming in Mel's stomach began to melt a little.

Just then, Emily ran in. "We have to go, Mel," she said. "I just overheard someone saying traffic is terrible. The highway is all backed up. You can't be late to your first day of JV practice!"

"Okay," Mel said. She smiled at Leslie. "Hope your leg starts feeling better soon," she said.

"Thanks," Leslie said. "Say hi to the team for me. Make me proud, Mel!"

Suddenly, the block of ice was back, even bigger than before.

Oh no, Mel thought. *What if we lose because of me? What if I ruin the team completely? Leslie will never speak to me again. All my chances of ever having a friend here will be gone — for good!*

· CHAPTER 4 ·

The Worst Practice Ever

The traffic on the road back to school was really bad. By the time Emily dropped Mel off at school, practice was starting.

Mel had to rush to get dressed. Coach Arnold shot her an annoyed look when she ran into the gym.

Mel hurried to grab a basketball and start shooting lay-ups. Then she saw Felicia looking at her and whispering to another girl.

After warming up as a big group, the freshman, JV, and varsity teams split up to practice separately. Mel started to go with the rest of the freshmen.

"Mel, wrong team!" Coach Arnold shouted. "You're on JV now, remember?"

"Oh, whoops!" Mel said. She turned back to her new team so fast that she almost tripped over her own feet. As she joined the group, she heard someone laughing. She tried to ignore it.

The block of ice from her visit to Leslie was still heavy in the pit of her stomach. Because she was shy and still new at school, Mel knew the faces and some of the names of her new teammates, but not much else. They were all sophomores and juniors, so Mel didn't even have classes with any of them.

"Hey, Mel!" said one of the girls. Her name was Katie, and Mel knew that she was a sophomore. Katie said, "Welcome to the JV team!" The rest of the older girls clapped and cheered.

Mel smiled. Everyone was looking at her. She could feel her face heating up.

"We're glad to have Mel on the team," Coach Arnold said. "Everyone, we have a lot of work to do today, so let's get going!" She clapped her hands, and the rest of the team ran to the end of the court.

Mel followed Katie. All of the older girls got started right away, forming three lines near the basket.

Oh, great, Mel thought. *Everyone knows what's going on except me.* The block of ice in Mel's stomach grew bigger.

The first drill was a three-person weave. *Okay*, Mel thought. *I know this one. I've done this a million times. I can do this.*

The girls finished forming the three lines. Mel was in the middle line, holding the ball. She passed the ball to Katie, who was on her right. Then she ran behind Katie and sped as fast as she could up the court.

Katie passed to Sara, the girl in the third line. Mel waited for the pass. Once she had the ball, she'd shoot a lay-up.

Sara passed the ball, and it fell into Mel's hands. Mel aimed and shot. But the ball bounced off the rim.

She looked up just in time to see the entire freshman team watching her. Her face got hot again.

"It's okay, Mel!" Katie called. But Mel didn't feel like it was. From the other end of the gym, she heard Felicia laughing.

Later, Mel stood next to Katie while the JV and freshman teams watched the varsity team run through a play. Once the varsity players finished, the JV team would practice the play.

"I don't get this play," Mel whispered.

Katie started to explain it to Mel, but Coach Arnold saw them talking. "Mel and Katie, show some respect and pay attention!" she yelled.

"Sorry, Coach," Katie and Mel said together.

Before Mel had time to learn how to run the play, the varsity coach called, "Mel, get in for Jill!"

Jill passed Mel the ball. Mel jogged over to Jill's starting position.

As soon as the play began, it was clear that Mel didn't know what to do. She passed the ball to the wrong person. Then she didn't move to the right spot.

Nothing worked right, and it was all because Mel didn't know what to do. She knew everyone would realize she hadn't been prepared.

The varsity coach blew her whistle. "This isn't working," she said. "Mel, you need to watch and learn what Jill does. Next time, know the plays, okay?"

"Okay, Coach," Mel said. She felt her face heating up. When she saw that the freshman players were all making fun of her, she felt even worse.

"Having fun, Mel?" Felicia asked, rolling her eyes. "Seems like the team would be better off without you. Leslie could play better with a broken leg than you can right now!"

Mel felt like crying. It was the worst practice ever.

· CHAPTER 5 ·

"Everybody Hates Me!"

All I want to do is finish my homework and go to bed, Mel thought that night when she got home.

She slammed the front door, ran to her room, and collapsed on her bed. But just then, she heard a knock on her closed bedroom door.

Mel was about to open her mouth to say that she just wanted to be left alone. Then her sister, Emily, walked in.

"I promise that I'll go away and leave you alone," she said. "I just need to tell Mom you're okay. She didn't want to bother you." Emily paused. Then she asked, "What happened at practice today?"

Mel curled up into a ball on her bed. "Everybody hates me!" she sobbed into her pillow.

Emily sat down in the desk chair next to Mel's bed. "Why would anybody hate you, Mel?" she asked.

Mel didn't know where to start. "Because I'm taking Leslie's place," she began. Then the words came in a rush. "And I'm not good enough to take her place. I don't know any of the plays, and Coach Arnold yelled at me because she thought I wasn't paying attention, and . . ."

Mel broke off into more sobs. Emily leaned over and gave her a hug. It took a long time for Mel to calm down and catch her breath. When she could finally talk again, she said, "Please don't tell Mom I was crying. She'll just worry."

"Get a good night's sleep," Emily said, standing up. "You'll feel better in the morning."

As she reached the doorway, she turned back to Mel. "You are good enough to play junior varsity, Mel," Emily said. "Don't let anybody tell you any differently. And don't tell yourself any differently."

· CHAPTER 6 ·
A New Friend

The next day, Mel couldn't stop thinking about last night's practice.

Maybe I was just imagining things, she thought. *Maybe Felicia wasn't laughing at me.* But she couldn't help thinking that being on the JV team was the worst idea of all time.

As she walked into the locker room after school, she heard a familiar voice. "Hi, Mel!" Katie called.

Mel's face brightened when she saw the older girl.

"Hi, Katie!" Mel said happily.

Katie walked with Mel to her locker. Mel stuffed her winter coat into the small locker and pulled out her uniform to get changed for practice.

"I'm so tired," Katie said. She yawned.

"I was just thinking the exact same thing!" Mel said. "It's been so hard to get out of bed in the morning lately."

"I know!" Katie said. "My dad always threatens to sing to me unless I wake up. He's awful!"

Both girls laughed. Then Mel asked the question she had been dying to ask someone since the night before.

"Is JV practice always that hard?" she asked quietly.

Katie smiled. "No way!" she said. "And anyway, yesterday was your first day practicing with the JV team. A couple of missed shots are no big deal."

"But I was terrible! And I got you into trouble with Coach Arnold," Mel argued. She sighed and added, "And I'm sure that everyone liked Leslie better than they like me."

"That's not true!" Katie said with a frown. "You were nervous last night. And Coach Arnold always yells. It doesn't mean we were in trouble." Katie thought for a second. "I think people just don't know you," she said.

"What do you mean?" Mel asked.

"You said everyone liked Leslie better," Katie explained. "I don't think that's true. I think it's just that you're new, and you're shy, and the rest of the team doesn't know you that well. Really. Today's practice will be better, and you'll love playing on JV. I promise."

By the time practice started, Mel felt a lot better. In fact, she felt like she had been friends with Katie forever. Yesterday's bad day seemed far away.

For the first time since she moved to Springfield, Mel felt like things were going to be okay.

· CHAPTER 7 ·
Try, Try Again

When the last bell of the day rang, Mel jumped out of her seat. She did not want to be late for practice again.

She ran down the hall, dodging the other students and teachers. In the locker room, she got dressed in record time. She quickly pulled on her practice clothes and slammed on her shoes. She was out of the locker room before any of the other players came in.

Mel was the first player in the gym. Coach Arnold was already there, setting up big orange cones for a dribbling drill. The cart full of basketballs was out.

After tying her shoes, Mel jogged over, grabbed a ball from the cart, and started shooting. Coach Arnold looked up from placing the orange cones and gave Mel a smile.

Just focus on shooting, Mel told herself. Coach Arnold always said players should put everything but the ball and the hoop out of their minds before taking a shot.

Mel concentrated hard on her shooting routine. Aim, shoot, follow through. She didn't notice as the gym started to fill up with other players. She didn't even hear Katie trying to get her attention.

Katie finally yelled, "Mel!" at the top of her lungs. Mel let out a small squeak of surprise. Her shot went wide and didn't even touch the net. Both girls laughed.

"Wow, Mel! You really had your game face on!" Katie said.

"I was concentrating!" Mel said. She passed the ball to Katie so that she could shoot, too.

Katie sank a shot from about ten feet away. "You should come over for dinner tonight," she said. "My dad always makes some really great pasta for dinner the night before a game."

"Really? That would be fun! I'd love to," said Mel, smiling.

"Cool," Katie said. "I borrowed my brother's car today, so I can drive us."

The two girls continued to shoot while the rest of the team trickled into the gym. The freshman girls all glared at Mel.

Mel noticed the glares. Her hands started to shake.

As the buzzer went off, signaling the official start of practice, Katie clapped Mel on the shoulder. "Just ignore them," Katie whispered.

The new friends started to jog their warm-up laps together. Mel was able to put the other players out of her mind, at least for a while. Now that she had Katie to talk to, it was much easier to ignore the other girls.

The first drill of practice was a shooting drill. The team formed two lines under the basket.

When she reached the front of the line, Mel passed the ball to a player in the other line. Then she ran around to receive her own pass for a shot. *Swish!*

Even though the spot to shoot from kept getting farther from the basket, Mel made almost all of her shots in the shooting drill. She felt great.

Then she looked over from the end of the line and saw Felicia. She was whispering and pointing at Mel. Like magic, the bad feeling returned to Mel's stomach.

Nothing I do will help, she thought sadly. *There's no point.*

· CHAPTER 8 ·

New Girl

Mel woke up a few minutes before her alarm clock went off the next morning. She got out of bed right away.

It was game day. That day's game against the Tigers would be her first time playing on the JV team, but she didn't want to get nervous. She knew if she was nervous, she wouldn't play her best. Since it was her first game, she wanted to do the best she could.

That morning at school, all Mel could think about was the game. She had to work hard to pay attention to her classes.

At lunch, Mel stood in line to get food. When Felicia and a bunch of other girls on the freshman team sat down at a table nearby, Mel smiled over at them. But they didn't smile back.

Instead, they all glared at her. Then they turned away, bent their heads together, and started whispering.

Suddenly, Felicia got up and walked over to Mel. She stood close to Mel and said, "You will never be as good as Leslie, so don't even try. Coach Arnold picked you because you're new. She felt sorry for you. She didn't pick you because you're good. You're not." She frowned and added, "Good luck tonight, new girl. You'll need it."

Before Mel could say anything, Felicia turned and walked back to her own table. The other girls were staring at Mel.

Mel didn't know what to say or do. She felt sick to her stomach. Just then, Katie got up and walked over to Mel.

"You have to ignore them," Katie said quietly. "I don't know what Felicia's problem is, but it's not your fault."

"I know," Mel said, but she didn't believe it. She wasn't looking forward to the game anymore. Not at all.

* * *

That night, Mel played her worst game ever.

It started with the jump ball. Katie was the tallest player, so she jumped for the Bears. She tipped the ball right to Mel.

Mel dropped the ball. The Tigers point guard picked it up right away and drove in to score.

On the next trip up the floor, Mel tried to play good defense. She tried to move her feet and stay between the Tigers point guard and the basket.

It didn't work. The other girl was so fast and such a good dribbler that she went right past Mel and scored again.

"Time out!" Coach Arnold called.

As Mel ran toward the bench, she saw Felicia in the stands. She was imitating Mel dropping the ball. All of the other freshman players were laughing.

For the rest of the game, the freshman team seemed to be thrilled whenever Mel made a mistake.

Mel could see them laughing every time she turned the ball over or missed a pass.

Felicia was right, Mel thought. *I will never be as good as Leslie.*

CHAPTER 9

Setting Goals

The next morning, Mel woke up feeling much better. Suddenly, she knew what to do. She didn't want Felicia and the other girls to be right, so she'd prove she was a good player and a good teammate.

There was another game that night, this time against the Lions. Mel set a few goals for the game.

First, she promised herself that she wouldn't let a mistake ruin her game.

Second, she promised to try her hardest, even if her team was losing.

Third, she promised to cheer the loudest of anyone for the freshman team during their game. Even for Felicia.

* * *

The freshman game that night went by in a flash. Mel's throat got sore from cheering. She pretended not to see the confused looks on the freshman players' faces when they saw her jumping up and down in the stands with Katie. Mel just cheered louder and louder.

The freshman team won, and Mel got ready to play in the JV game.

The jump ball went up. The Lions point guard chased the ball down and started to dribble to their basket for an easy shot.

Mel sprinted as hard as she could to catch up with her. She managed to hit the ball out of bounds. The Bears fans cheered loudly.

Mel smiled, but she remembered what Coach Arnold always said and tried to block everything out. She just focused on the game.

When there were only two minutes left, Coach Arnold called for a timeout. Then Mel glanced into the stands for the first time since the game started.

Mom and Emily were there, sitting a few rows from the top. Emily waved and smiled.

Then Mel saw that Leslie was there! She was sitting next to Felicia and a couple of other freshmen. They were all yelling, "Go, Mel!" as loudly as they could.

Mel shook her head in confusion. Could they really be cheering for her?

Don't lose your focus, she told herself.

The score was tied. Coach Arnold gave the team a few last-minute instructions. Then Mel and the rest of the team ran back onto the court.

The two teams traded baskets for a while. Then, when there were just three seconds left in the game, Katie was fouled.

Katie stepped up to the free-throw line. The gym was silent.

Then she shot, sinking the first free throw. The crowd screamed and cheered.

The official handed the ball back to Katie for the second free throw. She shot.

Swish!

The Lions passed the ball inbounds, but with only three seconds on the clock, their point guard couldn't get past Mel's defense to score. When the game was over, the Bears were up by two points. They'd won!

Mel looked up in the stands. Leslie and the freshman players were smiling and cheering.

Mel waved, and Leslie waved back. And to Mel's surprise, so did Felicia, with a huge grin on her face.

It worked! Mel thought. *I kept my promises, and my plan worked.*

· CHAPTER 10 ·
A Team

After the game, the team walked into
the locker room for their regular post-game
talk. Leslie joined them, using crutches to
help her get around.

Everyone was happy, smiling and
laughing. After a few minutes, Coach
Arnold called everyone together and asked
for quiet.

"Tonight was a really great effort from
all of you," Coach said proudly.

"I am really impressed with our free throws," she continued. Coach Arnold nodded at Katie and said, "Great job, Katie." Everyone clapped, and Mel put her arm around her friend.

Then Coach Arnold went on, "I am also very proud of our newest addition to the team. Nice job tonight, Mel!"

Everyone cheered. Mel could feel her face getting hot as she looked around at all of her smiling teammates.

She finally felt like part of the team, and the best part was that Leslie was there, cheering loudly.

When Coach Arnold was done talking, everyone hurried to change. They only had a few minutes before the varsity game would begin.

As Mel tied her shoes, Coach Arnold walked over. "Nice job," Coach said.

"Thanks, Coach," Mel said.

"And one more thing," Coach Arnold went on. "I talked to Katie. She seemed to think that some of the freshman girls have been giving you a hard time."

Mel looked down, embarrassed. "It's not a big deal," she said quietly. "I think it's over, anyway."

"I'm glad to hear it's over," Coach said. "But I'll still be talking to the freshman coach about it tomorrow. Mel, I know that you don't want to get anyone into trouble. But everyone here is on the same team, whether they're on the freshman team or JV or varsity."

"Okay," Mel said. "Got it."

"I know you do," Coach said. "Great job today. See you out there." She headed into the gym, and after a few seconds, Mel followed her.

Katie was sitting toward the top of the bleachers, and she waved when Mel walked in. Mel made her way into the stands to sit by her friend. But as she did, she heard a voice.

"Mel?" It was Felicia.

Mel felt a swoop of fear in her stomach. Had Coach Arnold already talked to Felicia? Did Felicia think Mel had told on her?

Felicia stepped quickly up the stairs to where Mel was standing. "Look, I'm really sorry about what I said the other day," Felicia said.

"Why did you do it?" Mel asked.

Felicia shook her head. "I was really upset that Leslie got hurt," she said. "I felt like you didn't care. It seemed like you were glad she was in an accident because it meant you got to play on the JV team." She sighed. "Plus, my dad gave me a hard time about not making JV. Anyway, Leslie told me that you were the first person to visit her in the hospital, and after I saw how you were cheering for us tonight, I realized I really screwed up."

"It's okay, Felicia. Really," said Mel. "Everyone says things they don't mean when they're upset."

Felicia gave her a small smile. "Thanks," she mumbled. "See you tomorrow." Then she started walking back down to the other freshman players.

Before Mel could head up the stairs, Felicia turned. "Do you and Katie want to sit with us?" she asked shyly.

Mel smiled. "For sure," she said. "I'd love that. We'll all sit together. As a team."

ABOUT THE AUTHOR

Val Priebe lives in St. Paul, Minnesota with four dogs, a cat named Cowboy, and a guy named Nick. Besides writing books, she loves to spend her time reading, knitting, cooking, and coaching basketball. Other books that Val has written in this series include *Full Court Dreams* and *Stolen Bases*.

ABOUT THE ILLUSTRATOR

Pulsar Studio is a collection of artists from Argentina who work to bring editorial projects to life. They work with companies from different parts of the world designing characters, short stories for children, textbooks, art for book covers, comics, licensed art, and more. Images are their means of expression.

GLOSSARY

addition (uh-DISH-uhn)—anything or anyone new

announce (uh-NOUNSS)—to say something publicly

contagious (kuhn-TAY-juhss)—spread by direct contact

decision (di-SIZH-uhn)—something you've made up your mind about

familiar (fuh-MIL-yur)—something you know well

goals (GOHLZ)—things that you want to achieve

ignore (ig-NOR)—to take no notice

realize (REE-uh-lize)—to become aware that something is true

regular (REG-yuh-lur)—usual or normal

tough (TUHF)—difficult to deal with or do

DISCUSSION QUESTIONS

1. Mel is nervous about her new role on the JV team. Have you ever tried something new that you were worried you might not be good at? Talk about how you got over your fear.

2. Why do you think Felicia was so mean to Mel in this book? Why did the other girls go along with her? Explain your answer.

3. What are some other ways Mel could have dealt with Felicia and the other girls? Discuss some possible options.

WRITING PROMPTS

1. When Mel needs someone to talk to, her older sister, Emily, is there for her. Who do you talk to when you have a problem or need advice? Write about that person.

2. What do you think happens when Leslie comes back to the JV team? Write a chapter that continues the story.

3. Mel sets goals for herself to help concentrate on the game. Have you ever come up with a strategy like this for yourself? Using Mel's idea, create some goals for yourself.

MORE ABOUT
WOMEN'S BASKETBALL

In 1892, a year after basketball was invented, women began playing basketball at Smith College, in Northampton, Massachusetts. Senda Berenson, a physical eduation teacher at the college, used the sport as a way to keep her students physically fit and active during the winter. Here are some other facts about the history of women's basketball:

- Early basketball hoops were actually peach baskets with the bottoms cut out.

- Basketball was originally played with a soccer ball.

- In the beginning, the court was divided into three sections, and each player was required to stay in their section.

- There were 6 to 9 players on a team, with 11 officials in early basketball games.

- The first intercollegiate game took place between Stanford and Berkeley in April 1896. Stanford won, 2-1.

- Men weren't allowed to watch women's basketball games in the beginning. Women were often assigned to guard doors and windows to keep men out.

- In 1936, a team of women called "The Red Heads" toured the United States, playing against men's teams, using men's rules. All members of the team were required to dye their hair red or wear a wig.

- Women had to play in skirts at first. This changed in 1896 when bloomers, a type of old-fashioned shorts, were introduced.

- Some of the most famous female basketball players are Babe Didrikson, Lisa Leslie, Rebecca Lobo, Candace Parker, and Sheryl Swoopes.